ACC. No: 07058090

SUPER CATS V

MAXIMUS FANG

Books by Gwyneth Rees

Super Cats
Super Cats v Maximus Fang

For older readers
Cherry Blossom Dreams
Earth to Daniel
The Honeymoon Sisters
Libby in the Middle
The Mum Hunt

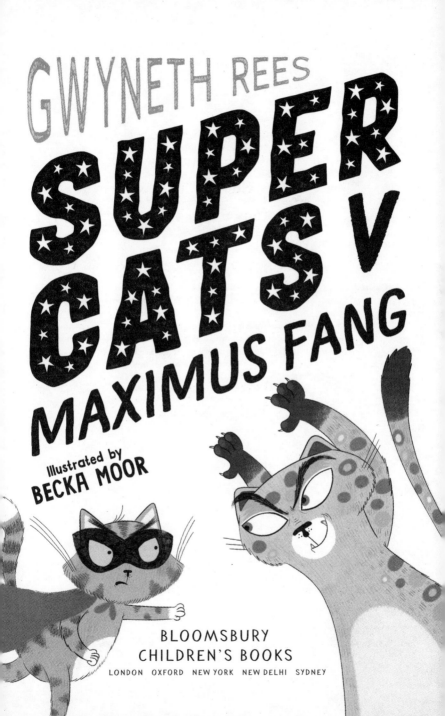

GWYNETH REES

SUPER CATS V

MAXIMUS FANG

Illustrated by
BECKA MOOR

BLOOMSBURY
CHILDREN'S BOOKS
LONDON OXFORD NEW YORK NEW DELHI SYDNEY

BLOOMSBURY CHILDREN'S BOOKS
Bloomsbury Publishing Plc
50 Bedford Square, London WC1B 3DP, UK

BLOOMSBURY, BLOOMSBURY CHILDREN'S BOOKS and the
Diana logo are trademarks of Bloomsbury Publishing Plc

First published in Great Britain in 2020 by Bloomsbury Publishing Plc

Text copyright © Gwyneth Rees, 2020
Illustrations copyright © Becka Moor, 2020

Gwyneth Rees and Becka Moor have asserted their rights under the Copyright, Designs
and Patents Act, 1988, to be identified as Author and Illustrator of this work

All rights reserved. No part of this publication may be reproduced or transmitted
in any form or by any means, electronic or mechanical, including photocopying,
recording, or any information storage or retrieval system, without prior
permission in writing from the publishers

A catalogue record for this book is available from the British Library

ISBN: PB: 978-1-4088-9422-4; eBook: 978-1-4088-9423-1

2 4 6 8 10 9 7 5 3 1

Printed and bound in Great Britain by CPI Group (UK) Ltd, Croydon CR0 4YY

To find out more about our authors and books visit www.bloomsbury.com
and sign up for our newsletters

For Rémy, with love

CHAPTER ONE

A NOT SO
PURR-FECT AGENT

Tagg swiftly scanned the alley for an escape route, his tabby tail bushing up as he realised it was a dead end.

'GET HIM!' yelled a gigantic bruiser of a ginger tom, the leader of the attack cats chasing him.

'Where'd he go?' another cat shouted as they rounded the corner of the alley.

'Those super cats are full of creepy tricks! Just stay alert!' said another of the attack cats.

Tagg was miffed. *Creepy tricks?* More like *awesome powers*!

Tagg's power was camouflage, which meant he could merge into his surroundings so completely that he almost became invisible. It was a super-useful skill for a secret agent.

As the attack cats moved further into the alley, Tagg's paw brushed against a dry leaf, making the tiniest of crackles. It was

enough for the ginger tom to swivel his head sharply and stare straight in his direction.

Uh-oh … The cat reached for the gun in his furry ginger holster, which he fired directly at Tagg! It was a splatter gun filled with bright blue paint that stuck to his fur, making his superpower useless. Seconds later, the three attack cats surrounded him, their claws unsheathed, ready to tear him to shreds.

A sharp mew came from behind Tagg, and with a sinking heart he turned to face his leader and commander, Topaz Top Cat.

'STAND DOWN!' ordered the portly grey female in her sternest miaow.

As her brilliant greeny-blue eyes fixed on Tagg, he squirmed. 'You're lucky this was only a training exercise, Agent Tagg!' Topaz scolded him, swishing her sleek tail in annoyance. 'Blind alleys do not make good escape routes. You should know that by now. And a good decoy does NOT end up DEAD unless it is absolutely necessary!'

'Sorry,' Tagg murmured.

'At least he led them away from me!' a cheery voice piped up from behind them. 'I got the microchipped goldfish safely back in our own fish pond, as ordered!'

'Sugarfoot!' Tagg exclaimed as his best friend and partner waved at him. Her fur was totally black, apart from one white paw. Her dainty appearance hid an unbelievably awesome superpower, for Sugarfoot had a super yowl that could deafen all living creatures for miles around, not to mention smash windows and crumble walls.

'Even if the mission was a success,' Topaz lectured Tagg sternly, 'this is the third time you've died this week. You should have activated your superpower *before* you dodged into the alley. Then the attack cats would have run straight past you.'

'Oh,' Tagg said. 'I didn't think.'

'A good agent *always* thinks,' Topaz scolded, her eyes flashing. She turned to the ginger tom and said in a clipped mew, 'There's a rather vicious sprinkler system in the garden across the road. Shove him under it, will you? I don't want him dripping paint all over HQ.'

Tagg was thoroughly drenched and shivering by the time he and Sugarfoot headed through the park to Super Cat Headquarters.

'Maybe I'm just not cut out to be a secret agent,' he said miserably.

'Don't let Topaz get to you, Tagg,' Sugarfoot tried to comfort him. 'She's just upset at the thought of having to tell your parents that something terrible has happened to you. You know the oldies go way back.'

Tagg's and Sugarfoot's parents were all super cats who had once worked alongside Topaz, catching villains and stopping bad guys. Superpowers ran in their families. Tagg's father, Chester, was super strong, and his mother, Melody, had super claws. Sugarfoot's parents had super speed and an incredibly powerful lick.

'Look who it is!' Sugarfoot suddenly mewed.

They had reached the abandoned park keeper's cottage that doubled as Topaz's headquarters, and outside – sharpening his

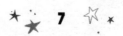

claws on a tree trunk – was Tagg's older brother, Rowdy. He was a stripy tabby cat like Tagg, but without the white tummy and tail tip. He had super strength like their dad, and he was also a member of Topaz's team.

'How are the new recruits then?' he called out. 'Topaz keeping you on your toes?' Without waiting for a response, he added, 'She sent me to fetch you – there's big news. Remember my mate Marshmallow, who's been working undercover with Hamish the hit cat and his gang? Well, he's brought us some important information. Come on.'

There was no time for any further discussion as Rowdy mewed a greeting to the two guard cats outside before taking them into HQ, where a meeting was in full swing.

'But their training isn't complete,' Topaz was saying, 'and Tagg is still not ready. For one thing, he's far too impulsive.'

'Nevertheless, they know the territory,' said a big white cat, who Tagg and Sugarfoot instantly recognised as Marshmallow. 'Hey, kids. How are you doing?' he greeted them.

'I know they made a good impression on Hamish, but they were only kittens back then,' Topaz said, ignoring the two youngsters as she continued her argument. 'He didn't see them as much of a threat, but things might be different now.'

Good impression? Tagg exchanged a puzzled look with Sugarfoot. What was Topaz talking about? Tagg thought back to the time he and Sugarfoot had gone to the woods looking for the hit cats.

Sugarfoot's dad was missing and they'd followed a clue to Hamish's hideout. The brief encounter they'd had there was terrifying – and they'd barely escaped with their nine lives!

'Hamish actually *liked* you two,' Marshmallow told them with a grin. 'He thought you had guts.'

'I suppose you'd better join the meeting,' Topaz said, waving them into the centre of the room. 'Marshmallow intercepted a message from Hamish's brother, Gory Gus.' There was a collective intake of breath at the news.

'Gory Gus?' Tagg just managed not to giggle at the silly name.

'Gory Gus is the worst type of killer cat,' Topaz said gravely. 'He loves the sight of blood and makes a horrible mess whenever he strikes. He's also a super cat with the power of telekinesis – which means he can move objects with his mind. Our organisation nearly caught him three years ago, but he escaped and fled the country on a plane bound for South America. He's just arrived back and is planning to break out his partner, Maximus Fang, from prison.'

'Maximus Fang?' questioned Tagg. He'd never heard that name either.

'He's a very powerful and evil super cat,' Topaz told them, 'which is why we cannot let Gus succeed. If they are reunited, there's no telling the chaos they could cause. It would be catastrophic. We need you to join Hamish's gang of killer hit cats and find out more about the plan.'

'But can't Marshmallow—' Sugarfoot began.

'I had to fake my own death to get out of there quickly,' Marshmallow interrupted. 'There's no going back for me. This mission will be all down to you!'

'But what makes you think he'll let *us* join his gang?' asked Tagg.

Topaz sighed. 'We're not completely sure, but Marshmallow is right. Hamish already likes you, so you're our best hope. I'm not happy about this but I don't see any other way. The mission will commence at nightfall tomorrow. Until then, Marshmallow will teach you everything he knows about being a hit cat, and Rowdy will coach you in working undercover.'

That afternoon Tagg and Sugarfoot learned lots of expressions for the art of killing.

Whereas Topaz's organisation tended to stick to rather formal words such as 'eliminated', 'neutralised' or 'terminated', in the hit-cat camp the phrases were far more colourful. A target could be totalled, zeroed, bumped off, bye-byed, taken out, done in, iced, dispatched, whacked, wasted, fish-sliced, cat-trayed or sent-to-the-dog-food-factory.

'But what if they don't believe us?' Tagg worried. 'What if they guess that we're just there to spy on them?'

'Well then,' Marshmallow said, 'you'd better give a convincing performance, because if Hamish suspects you're spies, you'll be fish food before you know it!'

Tagg growled under his breath. 'Fish food?'

'He means dead,' Rowdy said bluntly. 'The river that runs past the back of their den is the perfect place to get rid of bodies.'

Sugarfoot nodded solemnly but Tagg gulped. He just hoped he could pull this off.

The following evening, Tagg was resting at home, waiting for nightfall. His mother, Melody, was keen to feed him up, so there were ripped-open sachets of cat food all over the kitchen floor and their whole house smelt strongly of meaty chunks in jelly. Luckily, their humans were away for the weekend.

'We're so proud of you,' Melody purred as she gave Tagg a lick to smooth down the stubborn bit of fur on top of his head.

'We'll be even more proud if you come back alive,' said his father, Chester. 'Don't get too cocky – that's the main thing.'

'You just have to make sure you stay in character,' Rowdy added. 'You're a pair of tough wannabe murderers, so no getting distracted chasing butterflies.'

Before Tagg could protest that he wasn't a scatty kitten any more, he smelt a familiar pong and heard a wheeze as his great-uncle Bill limped into view, clutching a small furry object between his toothless jaws.

'Uncle Bill, you've actually caught a mouse.

Well … *half* a mouse,' Tagg corrected himself with a grin, inspecting what was left as his uncle dropped it to the floor.

'Took ages to catch the little blighter, scampering around everywhere … played havoc with my arthritis, it did,' the elderly cat complained.

'Uncle Bill, why don't you tell Tagg what you know about Gory Gus and Maximus Fang,' Melody prompted.

'Well, Maximus's power is weather control,' Uncle Bill began. 'After he got together with Gory Gus, the pair of them caused mayhem across the whole country. Storms, flooding, you name it. Humans, as well as thousands of cats, lost their homes, and any cat that tried to stop them was killed by lightning or sucked inside a tornado.

'Maximus and Gus were the most dangerous duo you could ever meet.'

'Uncle Bill was on the team that finally caught Maximus,' Melody said proudly. 'It was just before the last of his super teeth fell out. It's partly down to him that Maximus is safely locked up in Cat's End Prison, where he can't hurt anyone.'

'Cat's End Prison?' Tagg queried.

'It's a secret high-security underground prison where Maximus Fang is kept under lock and key. He has absolutely no exposure to the skies above, making him powerless,' Chester told him. 'It's built in an abandoned underground train station in Stoke Mewington.'

Tagg shuddered. 'Sounds horrible.'

Uncle Bill snorted dismissively. 'It's better

than he deserves. He's got his own exercise yard and poo plot, and plenty of evil pals to hang out with.'

'Tagg, it's nearly time for you to go and meet Sugarfoot,' Melody interrupted quickly, glancing out at the darkening sky. 'Now remember what we've told you – look after each other and don't take any unnecessary risks.'

Chester gave his son a lick. 'And use your head – not just your superpower. No matter how desperate things get, it's always worth taking a second to stop and *think*.'

CHAPTER TWO

AN UNDERCOVER MISSION

It was a few months since Tagg and Sugarfoot had first ventured to the hit cats' hideout. Back then they hadn't even developed their superpowers, and Tagg had only just learned that he belonged to a family of super cats. Now he was a secret agent on his very first mission. He couldn't believe how much had changed.

As the two friends picked out the path, guided only by moonlight, the thick woods were eerily quiet. They soon came to the first of the wooden signs Tagg remembered from last time. Written in bold Cat Scratch, it said:

Hamish's Hits
this way!

The 'Half-price Hits' special offer sign was gone, and when they reached a new sign, Tagg felt sure that the fees (in frozen fish or fresh mice) for Hamish's various services had gone up considerably. At the bottom it read:

Winter IOUs accepted
only if paying
in baby birds.

When they reached the spot where they'd first met Hamish, the two cats paused, uncertain what to do next. The path petered out and the moon had disappeared behind a cloud.

'Which way shall we go?' whispered Tagg.

'Shhh. Listen …' Sugarfoot's ears were twitching as she stood stock-still.

Tagg listened too and soon heard a low rumble. 'What is it? The river?'

'Maybe. Only one way to find out.' Sugarfoot pushed past him, heading towards the strange noise.

The mysterious sound grew louder and suddenly Tagg recognised it as the same noise he heard when he approached Uncle Bill's summer house during his naptime. 'Snoring!' he exclaimed.

The moon came out again just as they arrived at an opening between the trees. There, under a canopy of branches and leaves, the hit-cat gang lay sleeping all together, some resting their heads or outstretched paws on the cat next to them, while others curled up alone. They certainly didn't look the least bit dangerous.

'Well, well, well ... what have we here?' came a gruff voice from behind them, making them jump in fright.

'Lost our way in the woods, did we?' came another unfriendly miaow.

Before he could speak, Tagg was pounced on and thrown roughly to the ground, where he lay belly-up in submission. Sugarfoot hissed as she received the same treatment.

'Wait ... we only want to see Hamish!'

Tagg managed to shout. 'We want to join his gang!'

'WHAT'S ALL THE RACKET?' came an angry male voice with a strong Scottish accent.

'Intruders, boss. They're asking to see you.'

Hamish grunted crossly. 'How dare they! If they don't watch out I'll be the last thing they *ever* see!'

Tagg found himself trembling as an enormous grizzled tomcat emerged from the shadows. 'Who are you, laddie, and what are you doing here? You've got ten seconds to explain – and it'd better be good!'

'Yeah,' put in the thin grey cat who was holding Sugarfoot. 'You picked the wrong cat to wake up in the middle of the night, didn't he, boss?'

'Shut up, Kenny!'

As Hamish pushed his fearsome face closer to Tagg's, he growled, 'Don't I know you from somewhere?'

'W-w-we met you w-when we were l-looking for …' Tagg started to gag, partly from nerves and partly from the smell of Hamish's rotten breath.

'Looking for my dad,' Sugarfoot took over swiftly. 'You were right that Nemesissy shouldn't be trusted,' she continued, naming the super villain who Hamish had previously had a spat with.

'Wait – I *do* remember you two. You're the youngsters we caught romping about in my territory, bold as brass … all guts and no sense … that's what I said to Marshmallow …' Suddenly the fearsome cat's voice cracked with emotion and he ducked his head down and bit his own paw.

'Boss, you really shouldn't blame yourself for what happened to Marshmallow,' Kenny said.

'But I do! He was my right paw, my first lieutenant, my family … I should never have given him that whole sack of mice!'

'But you didn't know he'd eat them all in one go! Or go swimming straight afterwards! I mean, it's weird anyway – a cat going swimming, but—'

As if coming to his senses, Hamish turned his back on Kenny and growled fiercely, 'So what do you two want?'

'We want to join your gang,' said Tagg, trying to sound more confident than he felt.

'Oh, really?' laughed Hamish. 'Well, I don't take kindly to anyone disturbing my sleep, so you'd better hope I'm in a nicer mood when I wake up again in the morning!'

He grabbed Tagg and Sugarfoot by their scruffs and threw them to Kenny. 'Secure these two until morning. Then I'll decide what to do with them!'

At first light, Tagg and Sugarfoot were let out of their prison – a large, upturned wooden crate which two fat hit cats had been sleeping on all night. Hamish towered over them and snarled. 'Time for your job interviews, ya cheeky wee squirts!'

Tagg gulped. 'Interview?'

'Aye! You want to join my crew, don't you? Well, we're not some slipshod organisation that employs just anybody, you know. Now … come with me …' He gave Tagg a shove. 'Escort the young lady, lads!'

Tagg was led to the bank of a slow-flowing, murky-looking river, where Hamish pointed at an unstable rock overhanging the water. Remembering what Rowdy had said about this being the perfect dumping place for bodies, Tagg couldn't help shuddering.

Hamish was clearly enjoying Tagg's discomfort. 'Nothing like the prospect of a wee dip to focus the mind, eh?'

Tagg pulled a face. He didn't like water at the best of times, even though he could now swim – after being forced to learn in a local pond as part of his training with Topaz.

Taking a deep breath, Tagg jumped up to perch on the rock, steadying himself as it wobbled under his weight and trying not to look down at the water. He couldn't help noticing a stain on the rock just under his front paw. It was a browny-red colour. Could it be blood?

Behind Hamish, the other hit cats gathered to watch, pushing Sugarfoot to the front, where she would have a good view.

'OK,' Hamish said. 'First question …' He

paused dramatically. 'Why do you think I'd want a puny wee thing like *you* in my gang?'

'I ... err ... well, I can fit into small spaces ...' Tagg mumbled.

He hadn't reckoned on being so tongue-tied, or being tested on his knowledge of different murder methods in such detail. When Hamish asked him to describe a time when a killing had gone wrong and how he could have done better, Tagg started to talk about one of his less successful mouse-hunting experiences, only to be rudely interrupted.

'That's it! I've heard enough!' Hamish yowled impatiently. 'You've no skills to offer us! You're just not ruthless enough for this organisation, lad! Oh ... wait a minute ... one last question ... can you swim?'

Tagg heaved a sigh of relief. At last there

was something he could say to impress Hamish! 'Yes,' he mewed enthusiastically. 'I'm a very good swimmer, as a matter of fact!'

Hamish sighed. 'OK, we'll need to tie some weights to his feet before we push him in, lads.'

'WAIT!' Tagg panicked as two large muscly tomcats approached him, dragging chains attached to a lump of concrete.

But just at that moment, Kenny rushed over to Hamish with a scroll of paper in his jaws. The paper was spattered with blood and Kenny had a couple of bird feathers stuck to the side of his mouth. 'This just came for you by carrier pigeon, boss.'

Tagg and Sugarfoot were instantly forgotten as all the hit cats gathered round to hear the message.

'Is it from him, boss?' Kenny asked.

'Yes, it's from my brother, Gus,' Hamish confirmed.

'He wants to meet me tonight. I've to send the bird back with confirmation.'

'Oops,' Kenny mewed apologetically, letting out a burp that smelt unmistakably of fresh pigeon. 'Sorry, boss.'

'You haggis-head!' Hamish snapped. 'Go and catch another one. Gus needs to know it's safe to come out of hiding.' And he let out an angry hiss, as if he wasn't looking forward to the meeting at all.

He turned suddenly back to Tagg, who was still poised nervously on the rock. Hamish narrowed his eyes in a calculating stare.

'Actually,' he said, 'I think I'll keep you two. You might be of use to me after all ...'

After dinner Hamish ordered everyone to go to bed early. As soon as he set off into the woods to meet Gus, Tagg followed him, slipping out of the hit-cat camp and activating his superpower as he went. Sugarfoot agreed to stay behind to cover for him in case anyone noticed his absence.

Tagg easily tracked Hamish back through the woods until they reached the secret cat flap in the fence that led to the alley. Here Hamish stopped. Instead of going through the flap, he turned to his right and disappeared under a low bush growing against a high wall made of stones.

Tagg went to follow. At first, he could only see the wall in front of him, then he noticed that some of the stones jutted out to make a set of steps leading up to a small hole just big enough for a cat to slip through. On the other side he saw a small overgrown garden and a house. It was completely dark, apart from a single light in one of the upstairs windows. There was no sign of Hamish or his brother. Tentatively, Tagg crept across the damp grass, straining to hear any feline voices.

'SHOW YOURSELF!' came a sudden yowl.

Tagg almost jumped out of his skin. He threw himself to the ground, checking his fur and finding it indistinguishable from the grass he was lying in. Phew! At least his superpower hadn't failed him.

At that moment the moon came out from behind a cloud, revealing Hamish in the middle of the lawn, staring towards a large cherry tree.

Tagg saw a dark shape sitting on a branch halfway up the trunk. It was another cat –

similar in appearance to Hamish.

'No need to get yourself in a tizz, little brother.' The new cat spoke in a deep commanding miaow, which held just a trace of Scottish accent.

'Less of the little, Gus – I was born one minute after you,' Hamish grunted. 'Now let's get on with it! I'm a busy cat and I've a business to run.'

'Straight to the point as ever, I see,' Gus said. 'Listen up, I want you to break into Cat's End Prison and rescue Maximus. There's a secret tunnel that leads from Stoke Mewington railway station down to the old underground station where the prison is. The humans blocked up the tunnel when they closed down the underground platform, but dynamite will sort that out. Do you think your gang can handle it?'

'Of course we can,' Hamish grunted, 'but it'll have to be for the right price!'

Gus let out a furious growl as two beams of purple light shot from his eyes, hitting a tree directly behind Hamish. With a terrifying wrenching of earth and roots, the tree rose from the ground and was flung on top of Hamish, who screeched as he was whipped by its flailing branches.

'DON'T TEST ME, HAMISH!' Gus roared.

'I was only joking,' Hamish gasped, spluttering out a mouthful of leaves. 'You don't have to pay me anything. Just get this tree off me!'

Gus swiftly lifted the tree off his brother and dumped it on the ground. Hamish hissed under his breath as he limped closer to Gus, shaking his head to dislodge a leaf that was stuck in his ear. Still camouflaged, Tagg followed behind the pair as close as he dared, listening in to their conversation.

'I've a couple of new gang members who would be perfect for a dangerous job like this. I don't mind risking *their* necks,' Hamish said.

'That's the spirit!' Gus answered. 'So how soon can you be ready? I've checked the security rotas – the night shift has fewer guards.'

'Tomorrow night then?' Hamish suggested. 'That should give us enough time to prepare.'

'*And* time for Topaz to get wind of what we're up to,' Gus said. 'I say we act tonight!

It's still early. We've plenty of time.'

Hamish glanced up at the pitch-black sky. The moon seemed to have disappeared for good now. 'I suppose we could do it tonight,' he miaowed. 'If you're ready?'

'Of course I am! I'll leave the map and the dynamite wrapped in newspaper behind the bin to the left of the tunnel entrance. You can't miss it. Now listen carefully. Opposite the main entrance to the station there's a fish and chip shop with an alley round the back where they keep the bins. That's where I want you to bring Maximus. And don't let me down! Otherwise I might lose my temper again – and neither of us wants that!'

CHAPTER THREE

THE TUNNEL OF DOOM

Just a few hours later, Hamish and his gang were skulking in the shadows inside Stoke Mewington railway station. Hamish had mobilised his team so fast there had been no time for Tagg and Sugarfoot to get a message to Rowdy.

'The tunnel entrance is over there,' Hamish told Tagg and Sugarfoot, pointing his nose towards an iron grille across a darkened opening. 'The humans keep it locked, but Gus used his telekinesis to open the grille for us. It's only a small gap, but as you two aren't full-grown yet you should fit through easily.'

As it was the early hours of the morning, the station concourse was mostly empty of humans, but the gang still had to be careful in case a stray one in a blue uniform appeared.

The cats were busy studying the map of the underground tunnels. There was a large cross marking the point where the tunnel they had to enter connected with the old abandoned platform before it was bricked up. Tagg still found it hard to believe that the disused station platform had been turned into a high-security feline prison, and he could only imagine what the humans would say if they ever found out!

'What's that, boss?' Kenny asked, pointing at another area of the map.

'That's the main entrance to the prison – the one the guards use. It's an old emergency staircase that leads up to another iron grille at street level. It's always heavily guarded by Topaz's cats.'

Tagg pulled Sugarfoot to one side, whispering, 'It's not far. One of us could sneak away now and warn them.'

'It'll have to be you. You can use your camouflage,' Sugarfoot said. At the worried look on his face she added, 'I have my super yowl to protect me. I'll be fine. Go!'

The coast was clear, so Tagg seized his chance. He raced across the platform, heading for the cover of a large metal bin. A loud scratching sound from behind the bin made him stop in his tracks. It was Hamish, tidying up after weeing on a pile of empty crisp packets.

'What do you think *you're* doing?' Hamish hissed in his most threatening miaow.

Tagg just gaped at him. He'd done it again! He'd forgotten to activate his superpower *before* he made his move.

'Err … same as you …' he offered meekly.

'Get on with it then.'

'I can't with you watching,' Tagg said, hoping Hamish would agree to leave him alone for a minute or two.

'Need our privacy, do we?' Hamish teased. 'Well, you can wait until you're inside the tunnel in that case. Come on.'

Tagg and Sugarfoot easily squeezed through the gap where the metal grille had been slightly opened. According to Gus, Maximus's prison cell was directly behind the bricked-up wall. Their orders were to blast a hole in it and bring Maximus out through the tunnel.

Their hearts thumped as they headed along the passageway until they turned a corner and were out of sight of the entrance. Then they both stopped abruptly. They had each been forced to wear a horribly uncomfortable collar. A stick of dynamite was attached to Tagg's, while a box of matches dangled from Sugarfoot's.

Tagg was struggling to keep his tail from bushing up. He had to stay calm. He couldn't let his fear take over. Sugarfoot's throat was starting to tingle and she had to take deep breaths to control it. It wasn't the right time for a super yowl, even if she was feeling super scared.

'What are we going to do?' Sugarfoot whispered. 'We can't go back. Hamish and his gang will be waiting there. But we can't help Maximus escape either.'

'I know. If only we'd managed to update Rowdy and get a message to Topaz!'

Tagg frantically tried to think of a way to change the plan. 'What if we break into

Maximus's cell, but I stay camouflaged?' he suggested. 'You can pretend you're on your own and, while you distract him, I'll find the prison guards. I can tell them about the breakout and get them to alert Topaz.'

'That's a great idea,' Sugarfoot said enthusiastically. 'But I'm worried about using this dynamite. What if the whole tunnel caves in? I think it'll be safer if I use my super yowl.'

Tagg snorted. 'I think I'll take my chances with the dynamite!'

'I can control my super yowl much better now. Topaz taught me. I'll do a very *focused*, very *directed* sort of yowl … Come on! Let's take off these collars and dump them.'

'Well, if you're sure …' Tagg replied, quickly undoing his own, then Sugarfoot's.

★ ★ ★

The tunnels were dark and damp and seemed endless, but finally the two cats arrived at a fork, with one passage continuing around a bend and the other stopping abruptly at a grey wall made of different bricks to the rest of the tunnels. This was the wall they'd been searching for – the one they were meant to break through. According to Gus, Maximus's cell was located directly behind it. Tagg couldn't quite believe they were about to come face to face with one of the most dangerous criminals known to catkind. Or that he and Sugarfoot were completely on their own, with no backup whatsoever.

He stood well back, watching Sugarfoot cup her paws around her mouth as she focused directly on a specific section of the wall before releasing her yowl.

The sound grew steadily stronger, cracking bricks and sending old newspapers and other bits of rubbish billowing about. Soon Sugarfoot's yowl grew so loud and powerful that Tagg lost his footing and was blown back down the tunnel, just as he heard the sound of bricks smashing to the ground.

Sugarfoot had made a hole in the wall big enough for even the fattest of cats to squeeze through. She looked exhausted and it was clear that focusing her superpower in such a controlled way had used up most of her energy. But before Tagg had time to congratulate her, two huge leopard-spotted paws shot out of the hole and grabbed Sugarfoot by the throat. Tagg could only gasp in horror as his friend was pulled through the gap, head first.

Tagg only just remembered to activate his camouflage before scrambling through the hole after her. Inside, he found himself in a damp, dark prison cell that smelt strongly of cat wee. He stood completely still, staring at the cat who had grabbed Sugarfoot. He was easily the largest feline Tagg had ever seen – a spotted Bengal who resembled a leopard. Its massive paws were clamped over Sugarfoot's throat so that her super yowl was useless.

This was Maximus Fang – it had to be!

The ferocious cat flung Sugarfoot to the ground and stood over her as she croaked out. 'G-G-Gory Gus s-sent me.'

The big cat grunted. 'Why didn't you warn me before you knocked the wall down, you stupid fool?! I could've been hurt.'

'S-sorry,' Sugarfoot croaked. 'D-didn't think.'

As she spoke a disgusting smell wafted their way and Maximus pulled a face. 'Breakfast. They'll open the door in a second and chuck it in. You'd better keep out of sight.'

Tagg knew this was his chance. As soon as the cell door opened, he could slip through it, inform the guards and save the day! With a bit of luck, Topaz would have a team waiting for Maximus in the alley behind the fish and chip shop. They could capture not just him, but Gory Gus and Hamish and the hit cats at the same time!

Suddenly, the cell door was unlocked and a fat furry arm appeared, bearing a tray of congealed, foul-smelling food.

Maximus stepped backwards to hide the

ruined wall of his cell from view. 'Tripe and rotten vegetables. Yum – thanks,' he growled sarcastically.

As the guard grunted in response, Tagg seized his chance, slipping past Maximus to reach the doorway. But at the same moment, Maximus let out an angry snort and hurled the tray of food back at the guard.

Tagg yelped as the tray clipped his tail.

'What was that?' Maximus and the guard miaowed in unison.

Instantly, the guard reached for something dangling from his belt and pointed it inside the cell. It was a can of dog-wee spray. Concentrated dog

DOG WEE

HIGHLY TOXIC!!

wee was the vilest, foulest irritant known to catkind.

Without thinking, Tagg acted on impulse, diving at the guard and sinking his teeth into the arm that held the spray. The guard howled in pain, dropped the can and quickly slammed the cell door shut and locked it.

'I know you're in here, whoever you are!' Maximus hissed in Tagg's direction. 'I know you're a super cat too! Show yourself!'

Tagg didn't deactivate his superpower at that point, but then Maximus grabbed Sugarfoot by the throat again, and Tagg couldn't bear to watch her gasping for breath. Disabling his camouflage, he begged, 'Please don't hurt her.'

Maximus glared at Tagg, lifting a huge

paw and striking him on the nose. 'Who are you and what do you think you're doing?'

'Gus sent us to help rescue you. I just wanted to practise using my superpower, that's all. I didn't mean any harm!'

'How dare you mess with me, you little squirt! When I get above ground I could spin you in a tornado or trap you in ice so you never move again! Would you like that?'

'N-n-no! Please! We'll help you escape.'

'Yes, you *will*. And if you try and trick me again, I'll kill you both! Got it?'

'Please let my friend go!' Tagg pleaded as Sugarfoot gave a strangled whimper. 'You're choking her.'

Maximus gave out a savage growl as he dropped Sugarfoot and kicked her towards the hole in the wall. 'Now lead the way, you little brats, or I'll fish-slice you both right now and find my own way above ground!'

And, judging by the evil glint in his steely eyes, Tagg had no reason to doubt him.

CHAPTER FOUR

MAXIMUS FANG'S REVENGE

Tagg went first back through the underground tunnels, with Sugarfoot in the middle and Maximus at the rear to keep an eye on them both.

Tagg couldn't believe he was leading Maximus to safety – but he was sure Maximus would have killed Sugarfoot if he hadn't agreed. Anyway, it was too late, as the big Bengal was now close enough to the exit to sniff his way out without their help. As they neared the opening to the station, Maximus seemed to become more invigorated by the second.

'Yes! We're nearly there!' he announced triumphantly as they reached the last flight of steps. 'I can feel the sky! I can feel its pull on me! I can feel my powers returning!'

Loud miaows greeted them as they headed along the final tunnel to the metal grille across the entrance: 'It's them! They made it!' Hamish and the other hit cats were waiting for them on the other side.

'Change of plan,' Hamish grunted. 'The alley behind the fish and chip shop was blocked by a lorry. Gus used his superpower to dump it out on to the main road and now the place is swarming with screaming humans. We can't go that way!' As he spoke they heard the blare of human emergency sirens. 'Come on. There's another exit at the back of the station. Gus is waiting for us there.'

'This is our chance to escape,' Tagg whispered to Sugarfoot. 'Head for the exit with the sceaming humans and get ready to dodge them!'

As Tagg and Sugarfoot hurriedly slunk past all the police cars and fire engines they heard a clap of thunder and looked up to see a streak of lightning shoot across the sky.

'Do you think that's Maximus?' Tagg hissed.

Sugarfoot looked grim but didn't reply. She refused to look at Tagg as they headed back to Topaz's headquarters.

'Sugarfoot—' Tagg began nervously when they were almost there.

'You just had to mess everything up, didn't you?!' she spat angrily. 'You couldn't just stay camouflaged and keep quiet! Oh no! You had to bite that guard and give yourself away!'

'But … but he was going to spray the room with dog wee!'

'Which would have been foul – but we'd have survived. And then you could have got away to warn the guards and fetch Topaz. Now you've reunited the most diabolical super-cat team in all of history! There's no telling what they'll do now.'

'HEY!' A familiar voice made them glance ahead. It was Rowdy. He looked both surprised and relieved to see them. 'Thank goodness you're OK! We just heard about the prison breakout. What on earth happened? And why didn't you check in with any of us? We've been worried sick! We thought they must have rumbled you!'

'It's all my fault,' Tagg said miserably. 'I'm the one who let Maximus escape.'

Rowdy looked shocked, but as Tagg started to explain, he stopped him. 'You'd better come inside first. Topaz is going to want to hear this too.'

Tagg gulped. Now he was in for it – was he about to be fired? He didn't want to imagine not being on Topaz's team any more. And he couldn't bear the thought of not working with Sugarfoot. As he followed Rowdy inside he thought things couldn't possibly get any worse. But it turned out he was wrong.

After Tagg explained what had happened, Topaz gave him her most severe glare. But before she could respond, she was interrupted by crackling coming from the big screen that took up one whole wall.

Topaz looked perplexed, then suddenly Maximus's enormous face filled the screen.

He looked super smug. Tagg felt a shiver of dread run down his spine.

'Now it's YOUR turn to suffer, Topaz. You and all the cats who sent me to Cat's End Prison. Soon you'll wish you'd never messed with me. Gus and I have made you a little film show. Look – here we are visiting an old friend of yours in West Whiskerton.'

Tagg and Sugarfoot watched in dismay as the camera homed in on a car on a very windy street. In the back seat, two scared children were clutching a basket containing a large white cat. The car was swaying violently to and fro, when suddenly the driver's door flew off. There were loud screams as the woman grabbed her children and dragged them out of the car, leaving the cat inside. Seconds later, the vehicle rose up off the ground,

banging into lamp posts and nearby buildings. Gus was staring up at the car, shooting purple rays out of his crazed eyes.

Terrified humans were running for cover and sirens could be heard in the distance as thunder and lightning filled the sky. Maximus was out in the open, paws stretched upwards, growling as a whirl of debris engulfed the spinning car. The rapidly swirling corkscrew shot further upwards, and seconds later it was a tiny speck disappearing into the black storm clouds.

The film ended and Maximus's triumphant face came into view. 'Revenge is sweet!' he cackled. 'That was your friend Fingal Fatface– he was enjoying his retirement far too much for my liking! Now we're in the lovely seaside town of Cats Haven.

Apparently it's the perfect place for retired feline agents. Gus has located Charlie the Chop and Holly Christmas. Isn't he clever?'

'Who are they?' Sugarfoot asked.

Topaz's voice was croaky as she replied, 'Friends. Retired super cats. They were on the elite squad that captured Maximus Fang. Rowdy, we have to—'

But she was interrupted when a bulletin from the human news shot across the screen. A newsreader was speaking in a tense voice about the freak tornado that was raging above the seaside town of Cats Haven: 'HUNDREDS OF RESIDENTS HAVE BEEN EVACUATED AND A MOBILE HOME, THOUGHT TO CONTAIN AN ELDERLY LADY'S TWO CATS, HAS BEEN BLOWN OVER A CLIFF ...'

Maximus's face appeared on the screen again. 'Next stop Stoke Mewington,' he miaowed, continuing in a decidedly unhinged manner, 'I will soon rule the world! Only cats who serve *me* will be allowed to survive! Think ice storms! Think tsunamis! Think tornados and hurricanes! With my ability to control the weather and the incredible power at Gus's command there is no limit to the damage we can do! And there is NO WAY anyone can stop us!'

Then the screen went dark, and this time, mercifully, it stayed that way.

There was silence in the room for several minutes.

'I'm so sorry I let Maximus escape, ma'am,' Tagg mewed.

Topaz fixed him with a cool stare and said,

'It's my fault. I should never have sent you on that mission. You weren't ready.'

Tagg felt as if he'd been punched in the gut.

Sugarfoot spoke up urgently. 'There *has* to be some way of defeating Maximus and Gus before they destroy the world as we know it!'

To everyone's surprise, Topaz said crisply, 'There is.'

Even Rowdy looked shocked as he repeated, 'There is? Really? What do you mean, ma'am?'

'We still have the Weapon, Rowdy.'

'The Weapon? You don't mean—?'

'The weapon invented by Dr Specs. It's been hidden under lock and key ever since he was imprisoned in Cat's End for his treachery. I will order it to be delivered here immediately. It's the only way.' And she stalked out of the room with her tail held high.

As soon as she was out of earshot, Sugarfoot asked, 'What does she mean, Rowdy? Who is Dr Specs? And what weapon could be powerful enough to stop Maximus?'

Rowdy was almost too stunned to speak. 'Dr Specs is a scientist cat who used to work with Topaz. He invented a weapon that neutralises superpowers. Topaz was horrified when she found out what he had been working on and she ordered that it should never be used. But Specs disobeyed her. He was imprisoned and his weapon was locked away forever. Topaz said that such an invention must never see the light of day ever again.'

'Yikes!' Sugarfoot gasped.

'Exactly! And now she wants us to use it on Maximus Fang!'

CHAPTER FIVE

THE SECRET WEAPON

The freakish weather had the humans panicking so badly that the army had been called in to take control of Stoke Mewington, which was the next place to be attacked by Maximus Fang and Gory Gus. The thunderstorm was relentless, with high winds threatening to destroy everything in their path.

Tagg and Sugarfoot, together with Rowdy and Marshmallow, had snuck inside an army truck on its way to Stoke Mewington. The two older cats each had their front paws steadying an indestructible plastic tube that contained the neutralising weapon. Nobody had uttered a single mew since the phone signal was lost while Topaz was briefing them. Their normally fearless leader had sounded nervous as she'd told them, 'Maximus is threatening to cause a tornado in every town and city until the entire country is flattened. If he succeeds, many humans will die … even worse, many *cats* will die! We can't allow that to happen!'

Topaz had placed Rowdy and Marshmallow in charge, but Tagg had a crucial role to play in the mission. He didn't know whether to feel relieved or even more scared by this chance to redeem himself, especially now that they were totally cut off from HQ. But he WOULD NOT get it wrong this time!

'We're nearly there,' Sugarfoot mewed from her spot at the back of the truck. As the human vehicle slowed down the four cats jumped out, with Rowdy and Marshmallow keeping a firm hold on the Weapon.

Outside on the street, the wind was so strong they had trouble keeping their balance. Thankfully, there were no humans in sight as everyone had been ordered to stay inside.

Bits of guttering were swinging in the wind and loose slates were blowing off roofs and crashing down on the pavement as the gale raged on. Shop windows were blown in, and the local jeweller's had already been raided by some masked humans, while the fishmonger's had been robbed by a gang of feline delinquents.

'Maximus has got to be close by ...' Marshmallow gasped, panting as he dodged out of the way of a falling tree.

'I hope Topaz is right about this weapon,' Rowdy shouted back, barely audible above the howling wind. 'What if it's stopped working? It's been years since it was last used!'

The strange contraption didn't fire bullets – it released ultrasonic waves that disrupted superpowers. These waves didn't just temporarily rob cats of their super-powers – they removed them permanently. If they could aim the Weapon at Maximus and Gus and get a direct hit, they might be able to stop them once and for all. But first they had to get close enough without the evil duo realising what they were up to.

It wasn't going to be easy. Tagg felt as if

the lives of every cat in the country depended on them getting this right! They couldn't mess up!

Suddenly, a huge dark shadow fell over them, and out of the corner of his eye Tagg saw a wall beginning to topple. Sugarfoot was right next to him and he grabbed her by the scruff and yanked her backwards, just as a deluge of bricks came crashing down on the pavement in front of them.

Rowdy and Marshmallow weren't so lucky.

'Rowdy!' Tagg cried, as the dust blinded him.

Sugarfoot's entire coat was bristling with fear as she called out, 'Come on, Tagg! We have to help them!'

Marshmallow was lying down and licking at his back leg, wincing in pain. 'I think it's broken,' he said. Rowdy was unconscious, having been hit on the head by a brick, and a big lump was forming between his ears. Luckily, the Weapon, still in its special container, lay undamaged at his side.

Marshmallow hissed in a weak voice at Tagg, 'It's all down to you two now. Take the Weapon. Get Maximus Fang and Gory Gus. But be careful – *don't* point it at yourselves by accident.' And then he passed out.

Sugarfoot was instantly at Tagg's side, helping him roll the plastic container over the rubble.

'Even if we can work it, how are we going to get close enough to Maximus to use it on him?' she murmured. 'We don't even know—' She broke off as they suddenly heard a terrifying yowl, followed by a thunderclap so loud that the buildings around them shook.

'He's coming this way,' Sugarfoot said. 'Quick! We have to get you set up with the Weapon and find me a good hiding place.'

Tagg could still hear Maximus approaching. The terrible thunderclaps were getting closer and closer like a giant's footsteps, causing the ground to shake. Sugarfoot helped him set up the Weapon, then went to hide in the bushes. Tagg, his camouflage activated, lay on the ground sniper-like, his paw hovering above the trigger, ready to shoot.

The last thing Sugarfoot whispered was, 'Remember, Tagg – we only get one shot at this. If you don't wait for them to get close enough before you fire, you might not hit them. And then they'll know we're here and it'll all be over.'

Tagg's targets seemed even more like wildcats than before. Maximus Fang's leopard-spotted coat was shimmering, his eyes glowered with excited fury and his hiss was as spitty and ferocious as a serpent's, while Gory Gus's eyes burned with purple flames.

Worried that the fiendish twosome might spot Sugarfoot hidden in the bushes, Tagg's paw itched to press the trigger, but Maximus and Gus were still moving and he knew he had to wait until they were standing still.

As Maximus and Gus reached the pile of rubble, they stopped to take in the motionless bodies of Rowdy and Marshmallow before letting out triumphant growls. They surveyed the chaos all around them and purred loudly.

'First we destroy this pathetic little country,' began Gus.

'Then we take out the entire world!' finished Maximus. He began to laugh a truly evil and hideous laugh.

Tagg knew he had to act fast when Maximus reared up, pointing his front paws at the sky as if preparing to conduct an orchestra. Forks of lightning burst out of the black sky as Gus gazed up in excitement. The lightning began to strike at random – a tree, a lamp post, a block of flats. Soon there would be fires and casualties. Then Gus fixed his wicked purple gaze on the bush where Sugarfoot was hiding.

Just as a giant roll of thunder deafened everyone near and far, Tagg pointed the Weapon directly at the diabolical duo and fired.

Maximus let out a blood-curdling scream, his whole body shuddering as if in the throes of some kind of supernatural force, and then he collapsed in a heap on the ground. Next to him, Gus was propelled into the air. The purple fire drained from his eyes and he fell down beside his partner.

The thunder stopped in an instant and the lightning vanished. Suddenly, the winds dropped and daylight returned. The trees bent horizontal by the wind sprang upright again. Slowly, the eerie silence began to fill with normal sounds – birds chirping, leaves rustling, human sirens.

Tagg decamouflaged as Sugarfoot emerged from the bushes with four pairs of paw-cuffs, which she slipped on to the legs of the unconscious villains.

Rowdy was sitting up in the rubble, clutching his head and looking grumpy.

'Phone signal's back,' came a voice, and they saw Marshmallow waving the phone at them from behind a pile of bricks. 'Topaz says well done everyone, especially you, Tagg. She's sending reinforcements, and she wants us to take those two to Cat's End Prison on our way home.'

CHAPTER SIX

TWO TOP AGENTS

The following evening, back at Super Cat Headquarters, Tagg and Sugarfoot were standing in the middle of the room as the other cats congratulated them.

Topaz made a speech in which she commended her two newest recruits for their bravery.

'Maximus Fang is back in prison – minus

his superpower – and we've finally captured Gory Gus!' she declared proudly. 'And we have Tagg and Sugarfoot to thank for this!' She paused, tears gathering in the corners of her eyes as she added, 'Never in the battle of good against evil was so much owed by so many to just two – Tagg and Sugarfoot. You took on Maximus Fang and Gory Gus, and saved the lives of a whole nation!'

Cheers and caterwauls followed her announcement, and Tagg had to wriggle away from all the excited headbutts and nips he was getting. Marshmallow, his leg encased in bandages that perfectly complemented his fur, was lying next to Rowdy, whose head was also bandaged. Both were rather dopey from the painkillers the vet had given them, but that didn't stop them purring

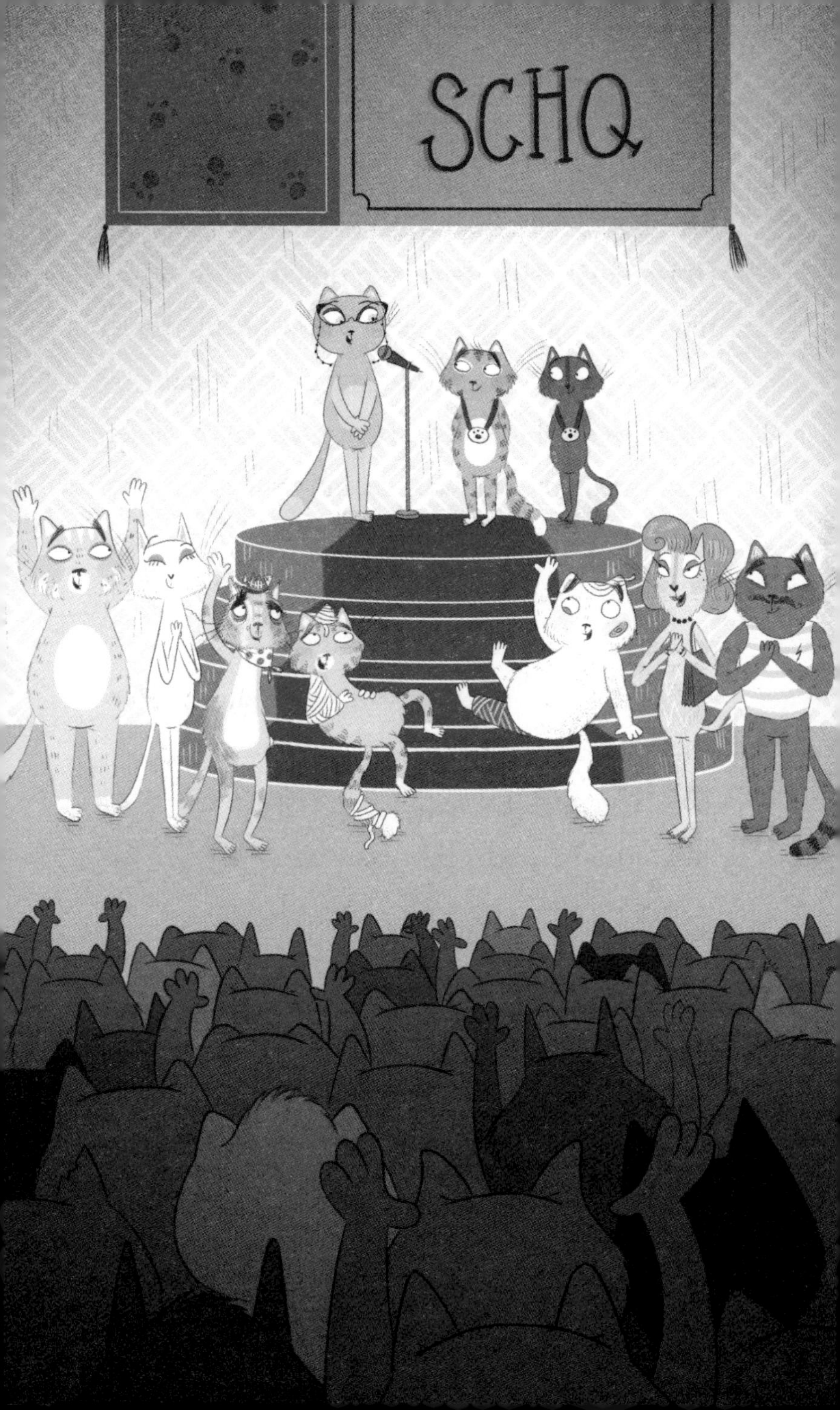
SCHQ

encouragingly as the two young cats were honoured. Tagg had worried about Rowdy and Marshmallow missing out on the glory, but they didn't seem the least bit put out that they hadn't been the ones to use the Weapon on Maximus and Gus.

And talking of the Weapon …

'Excuse me, ma'am,' Tagg addressed Topaz politely when all the cheering had died down, 'but where is the Weapon, and are we going to keep it?'

Topaz looked tense as she answered him. 'That's a very good question, Tagg. This weapon is so evil I've ordered that it be destroyed immediately.'

A deep-throated mew drew her attention as one of her advisers entered the room. 'A word, please, ma'am – in private.'

As Topaz left, Sugarfoot came skipping over. 'Guess what, Tagg? There's even more good news! Hamish has left town! His gang has broken up and they're not coming back!'

'Well, that *is* good news,' Tagg agreed. 'At least we don't have to worry about them finding out who we really were any more.'

Sugarfoot's expression changed abruptly as their leader returned to the room. 'What's up with Topaz?'

The look on Topaz's face made Tagg very worried. 'Maximus hasn't escaped again, has he?' he blurted out.

'No,' Topaz replied. 'Maximus Fang is still in prison, and so is Gory Gus. We don't have to worry about those two, Tagg. You've done a great job and whatever happens now, you mustn't forget that. We are all extremely proud of you.' She paused and Tagg held his breath, because he knew … he just *knew* … there was a 'but' coming – an especially big and especially bad sort of 'but'.

Topaz called for silence and waited for every cat's attention before making her announcement. 'I'm afraid I have to report some very serious news from Cat's End Prison. It seems that, in the chaos of the last few days, there has been another breakout.' She paused. 'Dr Specs has escaped.'

'The cat who invented the neutralising weapon we just used on Maximus and Gus?!' Tagg asked.

'Yes,' Topaz replied crisply. 'And it is vital that we recapture him as quickly as possible – before he builds another weapon, or invents something even more dangerous. I will need my top agents for this job!'

'Ma'am—' Rowdy and Marshmallow immediately started to volunteer their services, but Topaz swiftly interrupted them.

'You boys are in no state to return to the field just yet,' she told them firmly. She fixed her piercing gaze on her youngest agents. 'Tagg and Sugarfoot, this time I'm putting you two in charge. Don't let me down!'

MEET THE

MELODY

Superpower: Super claws!
Extremely sharp claws that can
cut through anything
Status: Inactive

CHESTER

Superpower: Super strength!
So strong he can jump huge
distances
Status: Inactive

TAGG

Superpower: Camouflage! Ability to
disguise himself to his surroundings,
making himself almost invisible
Status: Active agent

SUPER CATS!

SUGARFOOT

Superpower: Super yowl!
A yowl so deafening it can
shatter glass
Status: Active agent

ROWDY

Superpower: Super strength!
So strong he can hold up
crumbling buildings
Status: Active agent

UNCLE BILL

Superpower: Super teeth!
Incredibly sharp teeth that can
bite through anything
Codename: The Gnasher
Status: Retired. More suited to naps now

MEET THE

NEMESISSY

Superpower: Hypnosis!
Can bring any human under her power
and make them do her bidding
Status: Missing, presumed dead

MAXIMUS FANG

Superpower: Weather control!
Ability to create devastating storms
and strike lightning at will
Status: Locked up in Cat's End Prison

GORY GUS

Superpower: Telekinesis!
Can move any object with his mind.
Very dangerous!
Status: Locked up in Cat's End Prison

SUPER CATS!

MARSHMALLOW

Superpower: Unknown
Member of the Secret Super Cat
Agency, keeping cats everywhere safe
Status: Active agent

TOPAZ TOP CAT

Superpower: Unknown
In charge of the Secret Super Cat
Agency, keeping cats everywhere safe
Status: Active agent

HAMISH HIT CAT

Superpower: Unknown
Runs a deadly hit-cat service. Doesn't
need a superpower to be lethal!
Status: Missing, whereabouts unknown

COULD YOUR PET BE

SUPER?

Take this quick quiz!

1. Does your pet mostly ...
a) Sleep?
b) Play?
c) Spend time outdoors?

2. What does your pet like doing most?
a) Sleeping
b) Trying out new things
c) Getting into mischief

3. Does your pet have lots of friends?
a) No, it's quite solitary
b) Maybe. Certainly lots of different animals visit our garden
c) Yes! So many I lose track

4. Have you ever seen your pet do something incredible?

a) Not really, they just sleep a lot

b) Once I thought they had completely disappeared, but when I looked again they were right there ...

c) Yes! My pet once ran out of the garden so fast it burst through the fence!

Mostly a – Your pet might have had superpowers once, but they have probably retired now, like Uncle Bill

Mostly b – Your pet could have superpowers ... keep watching to see if any develop

Mostly c – Your pet definitely has superpowers! Wow!

HAVE YOU READ TAGG AND SUGARFOOT'S FIRST ADVENTURE?

OUT NOW!

Turn over for a sneak peek ...

CHAPTER ONE

A PURR-FECTLY ORDINARY FAMILY OF FELINES

Tagg was born in the spring – the first of five tabby kittens born to his mother, Melody, and father, Chester. It was Melody's second litter and this time she had her kittens in the family wardrobe, on top of her human's cleanest and most comfortable sweater.

Melody and Chester were fairly laid back when it came to kitten-rearing. Melody prided

herself on being able to lick a kitten spotless in two minutes flat, and Chester didn't bat an eyelid if one of his offspring tried to climb a tree or went to investigate next-door's cat flap without asking. All kittens got into trouble, he said – especially the adventurous ones. They either learned from their mistakes, or they lost their nine lives rather quickly.

'I know that sounds harsh,' Melody told the kittens, 'but your father is right.

The sooner you realise how perilous the outside world can be, the sooner you will learn not to do stupid or dangerous things.'

Tagg, who was a handsome tabby kitten with a white tummy, white paws and a thick stripy tail, glanced shyly at his father. All the kittens were in awe of Chester – a huge stocky ginger cat with dark green eyes. 'Did you do any stupid or dangerous things when you were young, Dad?' he asked curiously.

'I don't believe I did many *stupid* things,' Chester replied. '*Dangerous* perhaps – at least for an ordinary cat.'

'What sort of dangerous things?' Tagg was so excited to hear more that he forgot to ask what his father meant by 'ordinary'.

'Nothing you need to know about at the moment,' Melody told him swiftly.

As the months passed, Tagg noticed that his parents were treating him differently to the other kittens. He wouldn't say he was their *favourite* exactly, but he was certainly the one they scolded and fussed over the most, and he was always the one Chester took hunting.

It wasn't long before Tagg knew far more than his siblings about the arts of catching mice, stalking birds and correctly judging whether your prey would fit through the cat flap *before* you made a complete fool of yourself with a dead squirrel.

As Tagg approached six months of age, he was the only kitten of his litter still living with his parents, and it wasn't because no humans had wanted him. Twice Tagg had been rehomed to a new human household, and twice his parents had come that same night to retrieve him. Each time his father had carried him home by the scruff of his neck, until in the end their humans had given up and let him stay.

Tagg didn't really mind. He liked their comfortable home in its quiet, tree-lined street. He had a cat flap to come and go as he pleased, a plentiful supply of food and water

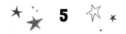

and a well-stocked fish pond in the garden (even if it was covered with an irritating metal mesh).

On his six-month birthday, Tagg was excited as he scampered out into the garden.

'Uncle Bill has caught a mouse for me to play with,' he called out to his parents, who were curled up together on the grass. Wild Bill, who was Tagg's great-uncle, lived on his own in the rickety summer house at the bottom of their garden.

'Wait, Tagg,' Chester said urgently. 'We need to talk to you.'

'Yes, Dad.' Tagg sat down obediently, hoping this wouldn't take too long. His great-uncle wasn't as sprightly as he used to be and Tagg was worried the elderly cat might not be able to stop his gift from scampering away if he didn't get there quickly. That was if Wild Bill could manage to refrain from eating it. After all, it was no secret that he was extremely partial to a bit of fresh mouse.

'Now that you are six months old, we want to tell you something about our family,' Melody began. 'It's a secret you must never repeat to anyone. Do you understand?'

Tagg's ears pricked up immediately. He loved secrets. 'Of course, Mum.'

'Good.' She looked at Chester to continue.

'Although your mother and I may seem like ordinary cats,' Chester began, 'we both have a very special ability. A *super* ability, if you like.'

'Wow!' Tagg was even more excited. 'Do you mean you have super*powers*?' His mother

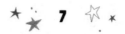

had often told him bedtime stories about cats with superpowers, but he had always assumed the adventures were made up.

'That is exactly what I mean,' Chester replied.

'Wow!' Tagg exclaimed again. 'So what can you do?' Maybe his mother and father could fly! Or turn invisible! That would explain how they were so good at creeping up on him whenever he was scratching at the carpet or stealing food from the kitchen table.

'Well ...' Chester sounded like he was making the most serious of announcements as he stated, 'your mother has extremely sharp claws.'

Tagg let out a spluttery mew of mirth. He couldn't help it.

Chester hissed. 'This is not a laughing matter!'

'Sorry.' Tagg struggled to get his face straight again as he stammered, 'It's just ... well ... surely ... don't *all* cats have those?'

'Allow me to demonstrate,' Melody said with a twinkle in her eye as she lifted one of her paws and stretched out the digits. Her claws seemed to go blurry for a few moments, then, all of a sudden, they changed into curved blades that radiated an odd, gleaming energy. The miniature swords looked totally unreal on the ends of her dainty white paws.'

Yikes!' Tagg blurted out. 'I mean, that's ... *awesome*!'

Melody turned around to face her kitten.

'My super claws will cut through anything, Tagg,' she said. 'And I mean *anything*.'

Tagg gulped. Looking nervously at his father, he asked, 'So what can you do, Dad?'

Chester crouched down on his back legs and began to swing his hindquarters like any cat preparing to spring. But then he leaped off the ground and up, up, up, as high as the roof of the house and right over it.

Tagg raced around to the front of the house as fast as he could, but by the time he got there his father had vanished. 'Where is he?' Tagg mewed in wonder as he searched the sky.

'Oh … several streets away by now, I expect,' Melody replied as she joined him. 'His back legs are *extremely* powerful.' She gave Tagg's head a gentle lick. 'I know it's a lot to take in, but don't worry. You'll be used to the idea by the time your own power develops.'

'M-my own p-power … ?' Tagg gasped.

'That's right. You might have super claws or super strength, or you may develop something completely different. Whatever your power is, your father and I will be here to teach you how to use it properly. That is why we couldn't let you leave us like your brothers and sisters.'

Tagg suddenly thought of something. 'But how come *I'm* the only one? What makes *me* so special?'

'Nobody knows why only one kitten in each litter is born with superpowers,' Melody explained. 'But I *knew* you were the one from the moment you were born.

It was exactly how I felt when your brother Rowdy was born. He was the super kitten from our first litter.'

'Rowdy?' It was the first time Tagg had heard the name. 'What superpower does he have? Where is he now?'

'He decided that he wanted to go off on his own and explore other places. He has super strength, like Chester.' Her voice was light but Tagg thought she looked sad. 'Now, didn't you say something about a mouse?'

'Oh yes … wait … does Uncle Bill know about this?'

'Of course. He's a super cat too – at least he *was*.'

'Really?' Tagg immediately thought of the impressive stench of cat wee in the summer house. His mother had told him that it was just as well Uncle Bill's wee was so powerful because it meant any strange cats steered well clear. Tagg asked uncertainly, 'So does he have super *wee*?'

Melody let out a little snort. 'Of course not. His wee is quite ordinary, believe it or not. There's nothing unusual about a male cat spraying his territory, though your uncle does take it a bit far. No ... Wild Bill had super *teeth*. They could bite through anything – glass, wood, metal, vets' instruments ... And if he clamped on to something – or some- body – there wasn't anything you could do to shake him loose!'

'Wow! That sounds *mega* awesome.'

'It was. Unfortunately, all his teeth have fallen out now and he has no superpower left. And speaking of Uncle Bill ...'

'I'd better go!' Tagg gasped, suddenly thinking of his promised mouse.

'Make sure you eat it all up afterwards, Tagg,' his mother reminded him. 'You know how I feel about cats who only *play* with their food.'

Tagg found his great-uncle sitting outside the summer-house door, thoroughly washing his whiskers.

'Oh no,' Tagg miaowed crossly. 'You've eaten it already, haven't you?'

The older cat looked up and gave him a calm blink. 'I most certainly have, young fella. Fresh mouse can be extremely hard to resist if you're that way inclined. That's why I told you to come straight away. Now off you go while I take my nap.' Wild Bill napped after every meal these days, saying that at his age he couldn't be expected to digest food *and* stay awake at the same time.

Looking at his great-uncle now, Tagg found it hard to believe that the elderly tabby cat with absent teeth and patchy fur had once been a super cat.

He couldn't keep the excitement from his voice as he blurted, 'Mum and Dad just told me about their superpowers!'

'Time you knew,' the older cat grunted matter-of-factly. 'So how does it feel to be the son of Feline Force One?'

'Feline Force One?' Tagg asked.

'That was their secret-agent code name. Of course, there were others – Feline Force Two, Feline Force Three, Feline Force Four and such like. Me – I always worked alone.

My code name was The Gnasher.' He gave a purr of pride.

'Wait – you were *secret agents*?' Tagg wondered what other information his parents had left out.

'That's right. Our boss, the top cat, was called Topaz. She lived at HH with the leader of the humans.'

'HH?' Tagg asked.

'Human Headquarters. It's in the middle of the biggest human city. Anyway, the top human at the time was a real cat lover and he often talked to Topaz about his worries. She learned about all the problems in this country, and that's how we got our missions. When a different human leader came into power, Topaz was prepared to stay and help her too, only this one was allergic to cats and she found herself banished.'

'That's terrible!'

'It certainly was. Topaz was forced to close down the whole operation. After that we moved here. Your parents had kittens and I lost my last few teeth.' He belched and Tagg caught a strong whiff of freshly devoured mouse.

'Mum told me about Rowdy,' Tagg said.

Wild Bill grunted. 'Too headstrong for his

LOOK OUT FOR

SUPER CATS

V Dr Specs

COMING SOON!

GWYNETH REES

Gwyneth Rees is half Welsh and half English and
grew up in Scotland. She studied medicine and qualified
as a doctor before she became a full-time writer.
She lives near London with her husband,
two young daughters and one noisy cat.

BECKA MOOR

Becka Moor is a children's book illustrator and storyteller living in Manchester. You can find her illustrations in a variety of fiction books and series as well as picture books. She has an obsession with cats and loves anything a bit on the quirky side.